We Will Win!

HAILEY SCRAGG • LISA PERRETT

Carson Dellosa Education®

Pip and Kit sit and sip.

Can we hit the bin?

I am big.

I will win!

وِيع!

I can rig the win!

Zip!

We did miss the bin.

We can fix it.

We will win!

We did it!

We hit it in!

HiT!!

big	it	sit
bin	Kit	will
did	miss	win
fix	Pip	zig
hit	rig	zip
in	sip	

Decodable Words

am

can

High-Frequency Words

and	the
I	we